To my mum and dad,
and James

M

Published in 2000 by The Millbrook Press, Inc.,
2 Old New Milford Road, Brookfield, Connecticut 06804
www.millbrookpress.com

First published in Great Britain in 1999 by Bloomsbury Publishing Plc
38 Soho Square, London W1V 5DF

Library of Congress Cataloging-in-Publication Data

Gosney, Joy.
  Naughty Parents / Joy Gosney
    p. cm.
  Summary: A child's parents are very naughty in the park, getting dirty, splashing in
puddles, and dribbling ice cream
  ISBN 0-7613-1823-2 (lib. bdg.) -- ISBN 0-7613-1341-9 (trade)
  [1.Parent and child--Fiction. 2. Behavior--Fiction. 3. Parks--Fiction.] I. Title

PZ7.G677 Nau 2000
[E]--dc21

99-037398

Designed by Dawn Apperley
Printed and bound in Hong Kong, China
1 3 5 7 9 10 8 6 4 2

Naughty Parents

Joy Gosney

THE MILLBROOK PRESS   BROOKFIELD, CONNECTICUT

I love Mom and Dad, but they do like getting into mischief.

So when they said we were going to the park to see the ducks, I knew I would have to keep a sharp eye on them.

And, just as I thought, as soon
as we reached the duck pond,
Mom and Dad took off!

They ran off to play . . . and got lost!

"I can't find my naughty parents anywhere!" I told the ducks. "What shall I do?"

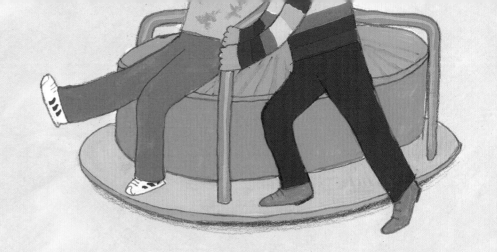

"We saw them running toward the playground," they said. "You might find them there."

"Whee!"
"Awesome!"

When I got to the playground,
I saw a nice lady.
"Have you seen my naughty parents?"
I asked.
"Yes, I saw them sliding down the
slide—and they were getting very
dirty!" said the lady. "And then they
went that way."
But I couldn't see them anywhere.

They had already run off . . .

. . . to find some puddles.

I hurried on until I met a grumpy man. "Have you seen my naughty parents?" I asked.

"Oh yes! I saw them jumping in puddles and they got me all wet!" said the man.
But I couldn't see them anywhere.

They had already run off . . .

. . . to buy ice-cream cones.

I hurried after my naughty parents
until I saw a kind woman.
"Have you seen my naughty parents?"
I asked.
"I did, and they were eating sticky
ice cream!" said the woman.
But I still couldn't see them anywhere.

They had already run off.

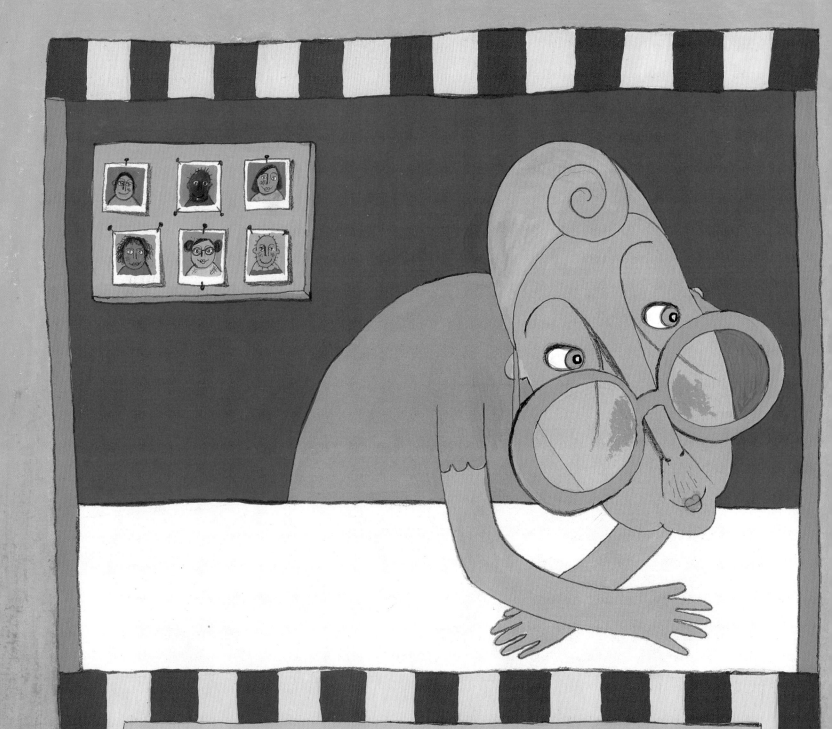

By now I was getting worried, so I went straight to the Missing Parents Booth and asked the lady if she had any **very dirty, wet,** and **sticky** parents. "Ah yes!" she said. "I have two parents here who fit that description. They must belong to you!"

At last I had found them!
Since that day, Mom and Dad have
never once run off and gotten lost . . .

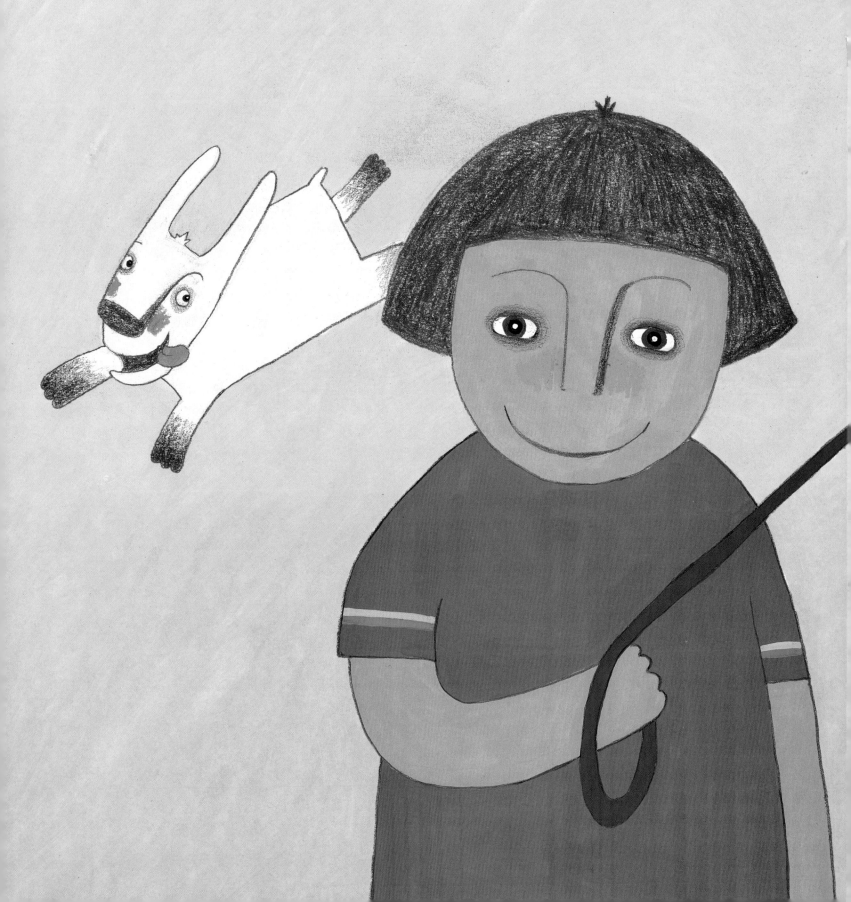

. . . and I know why!